Wish Upon a Pet

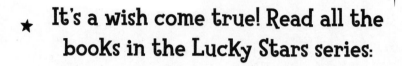

It's a wish come true! Read all the books in the Lucky Stars series:

Wish Upon a Pet

by Phoebe Bright
illustrated by Karen Donnelly

SCHOLASTIC INC.

NEW YORK TORONTO LONDON AUCKLAND
SYDNEY MEXICO CITY NEW DELHI HONG KONG

For Tom and Zara Scott, with love
Special thanks to Valerie Wilding

ISBN 978-0-545-41999-4

Text copyright © 2012 by Working Partners Limited
Cover art copyright © 2012 by Scholastic Inc.
Interior art copyright © 2012 by Karen Donnelly

12 11 10 9 8 7 6 5 4 3 2 1   12 13 14 15 16 17/0

Printed in China   68
First Scholastic printing, August 2012

Lucky Star that shines so bright,
Who will need your help tonight?
Light up the sky, and thanks to you
Wishes really do come true. . . .

Whimsy
Woods

Strawberry
Field

Flashley Manor Hotel

Cake Shop

Costume
Shop

Bert's Donkey
Stables

Pier

Hello, friend!

I'm Stella Starkeeper, and I want to tell you a secret. Have you ever gazed up at the stars and thought that they could be full of magic? Well, you're right. Stars really are magical!

Their precious starlight allows me to fly down from the sky. I'm always on the lookout for boys and girls who are especially kind and helpful. I train them to become Lucky Stars—people who can make wishes come true!

So the next time you're under the twinkling night sky, look out for me. I'll be floating among the stars somewhere.

Give me a wave!

Love,

Stella Starkeeper

* 1 *
Stella Starkeeper

"Wow! That wind is strong!" Cassie said. She laughed as a star-patterned pillowcase blew off the clothesline and into her face.

The two charms on Cassie's silver bracelet jangled as she hung the pillowcase back on the line. She glanced at the charms — a tiny bird and a crescent moon — and smiled. Their magic helped her make special wishes come true! *I hope I meet someone with a wish today*, she thought.

"When we offered to help your mom hang up the laundry, I didn't expect to have to chase it around the yard!" called her friend Alex.

Cassie looked up to see him collecting three socks that had blown into an apple tree. She laughed.

"How many towels do you have?" asked Alex, hanging up the socks and looking around. "I've already hung up eight. That's about a third of what's here, so I calculate . . ." He mumbled to himself for a minute, frowning in concentration.

Cassie giggled. Alex loved math and

science, and was always trying to solve things with an equation or formula. "Remember, this is a B&B," she said. "That means we have ten times more towels than an ordinary house."

Starwatcher Towers was far from ordinary. That's why Cassie loved living there! One part of it was a bed-and-breakfast, where all different guests came to stay. The other part was an observatory where Cassie's dad worked, watching the stars and planets in the night sky. Cassie's bedroom even had a glass ceiling, so she could lie in bed watching the stars!

"You shouldn't really be helping," said Cassie. "B&B guests don't normally hang their own towels."

Alex shrugged. "Mom and Dad are meeting someone today, so I'm happy to have something to do. Anyway," he said shyly, "it's nice to help friends, isn't it?"

Cassie grinned. "You bet!"

She hadn't been too sure about Alex when he first arrived at Starwatcher Towers. He'd been awfully quiet! Then she realized he only seemed unfriendly because he was shy, and they soon became good pals.

The cat flap in the back door clattered. Out ran Alex's fluffy white puppy, Comet, followed by Cassie's cat, Twinkle. The pets had become friends, too—just like Cassie and Alex!

Cassie stroked Twinkle's black fur.

"*Meowwww,*" he yowled.

"*Ruff!*" barked Comet.

Cassie brushed her long hair out of her eyes. "You two should stay inside," she told the animals. "You might blow away!"

"Only if the wind's strong enough," said Alex, stroking his chin. "I'll get my anemometer, so I can measure the wind speed." He ran inside. The wind banged the door shut behind him.

Cassie threw another towel over the line. As she held it down with a clothespin, she noticed a bright light shining through the clouds overhead. *Is that a star?* Cassie wondered. *In the morning?*

Cassie's dad had taught her a lot about the stars. She knew that you couldn't usually see them in the daytime, because the sun was too bright. But as she watched, this star seemed to be whirling down toward her!

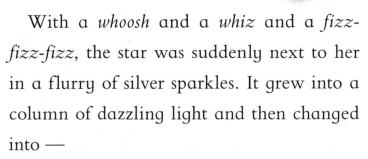

Cassie remembered the last time she saw a star doing something like that. Could it be . . . ?

With a *whoosh* and a *whiz* and a *fizz-fizz-fizz*, the star was suddenly next to her in a flurry of silver sparkles. It grew into a column of dazzling light and then changed into —

"Stella Starkeeper!" cried Cassie. "You're back."

A beautiful young woman stood before her in a short silver dress and a shiny silver jacket with star-shaped buttons. She wore glittery leggings and silver boots, and carried a wand that was tipped with a shining star. Her hair fluttered in the wind. A crown woven from strands of glistening silver sat on top of her head.

Stella's velvety blue eyes twinkled like stars in the night sky. "Hello, Cassie," she said, smiling kindly. "I came to see how you're doing with your new charm."

The charm bracelet was Stella's gift to Cassie on her seventh birthday, a few days ago. Now Stella touched Cassie's bracelet with her wand, and a sprinkle of sparkles drifted to the grass.

"Don't forget," Stella said, "you must listen for someone to make a special wish, and use the powers of your magic charms to help make the wish come true. Then you'll earn a new magic charm."

"When I earn seven charms, I'll be a real Lucky Star, just like you," said Cassie.

Stella Starkeeper smiled. "And you'll be able to grant wishes whenever you like. You won't even have to wait for anyone to tell you their wish!"

Cassie glanced at her bracelet. "The bird charm gives me the power to fly," she said, "but what does my moon charm do? I don't feel any different."

★ ✳ ★ ✳

Stella's eyes sparkled, and her crown glittered as she leaned forward. "Listen carefully, Cassie," she whispered. "You might hear something you never expected."

Then, with a wave of her wand, Stella faded into a silvery mist. But as she disappeared, a sudden gust of wind blew her silver crown off!

"Wait!" cried Cassie.

It was too late. Stella was gone.

Cassie chased the crown as it tumbled over and over on the grass. She reached out to grab it, but it bounced against a tree, soared over the fence, and rolled down the hill.

She watched in despair.

★　　✳　　★　　✳

"Found it!" yelled Alex just then.

Cassie turned. He was holding one of his science contraptions. "Oh," she said. "Is that your amin . . . namen . . . ?"

Alex grinned. "An-em-o-meter," he said.

"Anen . . ." Cassie began. Then she laughed. "Your wind-speed measurer!"

She watched Alex put the anemometer on the picnic table. It had a stand with four arms, and each had a cup shape at the end. The wind blew the cups around and around.

★ ✳ ★ ✳

As Alex tinkered with the machine, Cassie remembered what Stella had said. She wandered over to lean against the plum tree's knobby trunk. Then she closed her eyes, thought about her crescent moon charm, and listened.

A voice came from behind her.

"This wind's blowing my coat all over the place," it said. "I must look like a total mess."

It was a weird, yowly sort of voice. Cassie was sure she'd heard it before . . . but where?

She opened her eyes. It definitely wasn't Alex talking, but no one else was around. She could only see Comet, who was playing on the other side of the yard, and Twinkle, who was sitting next to Cassie and staring up at her with wide amber eyes.

Cassie gasped. *"Twinkle?"*

2
Sunbeam and Sita

Cassie knelt down. Magical sparkles danced around her cat, making his whiskers twitch.

Twinkle looked straight back at her. "I'm scruffy, aren't I?" he asked.

"N-no," Cassie stammered. She couldn't believe her ears!

The cat's eyes widened. "You're talking to me," he said.

"And you're talking to me!" said Cassie. "Alex! Come here!"

★ ✳ ★ ✳

Alex ran over and knelt down.

"Twinkle," said Cassie, "speak to Alex."

"Hello," said the cat. "Cassie can understand me. Can you?"

"Did you hear him speak?" asked Cassie.

"Of course I did," replied Alex. "*Meow, meow, meow.* What were you expecting?" He shrugged and headed back to his anemometer.

Twinkle looked at Cassie. "I'll tell Comet you talked to me. He'll be so jealous!" He prowled over to Comet. Sparkles danced in the air around both of them.

"Why is Twinkle staring at Comet's tail?" Alex wondered aloud. "And why is Comet barking like that?"

"They're talking!" answered Cassie. "Comet's saying, 'Watch my tail, Twinkle. The wind's whipping it back and forth without me wagging it!'"

Alex spun around and looked at her with wide eyes. "You can *understand* him?"

Cassie nodded, realizing that this must be the power of her crescent moon charm. *How exciting! I've always wanted to talk to Twinkle,* she thought. *Now I can!*

"But it's not possible," Alex said.

Twinkle was curling himself around Cassie's legs, saying, "I love being able to talk to you. It's *grrrreat!*"

Alex grinned. "He's purring now. I guess you can understand that, too?"

"Yes," said Cassie. "He says that he's happy he can talk to me."

Alex stroked his chin. "Hmmm. You're probably just watching their behavior, and that helps you understand them," he said.

How can I prove that I know what the pets are saying? Cassie wondered. Then she had an idea.

"Comet," she said. "Tell me something that you and Alex do when you're by yourselves."

The dog wagged his tail excitedly. "Every

morning," said Comet, "I jump on his bed and lick his ear. Then he hides under the covers."

Cassie smiled and turned to Alex. "Comet wakes you up by licking your ear."

Alex gaped at her. "You *can* understand animals!" He scratched his head. "But there must be a scientific explanation."

Cassie threw a ball for Comet. He barked, "Whoopee!" and chased after it.

"You scientists are supposed to be good at observing things," said Cassie, smiling at Alex. "Don't you recognize magic when it's right in front of you?"

Comet brought the ball back. "Again! Again!" he panted.

Cassie tossed the ball and turned to

her friend. "Alex," she said, "I told you about Stella Starkeeper and my bracelet's power." She jangled the charms. "Don't you remember flying in the sky with me, looking at the clouds?"

He nodded. "Yeahhh, but I still think there's a scientific —" He stopped, because Cassie was gazing past him. "You're not listening!"

"Sorry," said Cassie. "I just noticed some people visiting Bert." She pointed down the hill that led into the town of Astral-on-Sea. A big green truck towing a horse trailer was pulling into Bert's stables. His donkeys lived at the stables when they weren't giving children rides on the beach.

"Let's go and see what's happening,"

Cassie went on. She wondered if she could understand horses, too.

They ran down the hill, with the wind pushing them forward. The stables were way down at the bottom, close to the sandy beach.

★　　✳　　★　　✳

"The wind's helping us!" Alex cried.

"It's so strong!" Cassie shrieked.

"That's just what my anemometer measurements showed," Alex puffed as they rounded the corner by the stables.

Cassie paused at Bert's gate. A girl about her age was leading a pretty pony out of the horse trailer. The donkeys watched curiously. Even Coco, the new, timid donkey, peered over his stable door. Cassie was glad that he was getting braver.

★ ✳ ★ ✳

The girl's mom chatted with Bert as she unpacked the pony's equipment. Then she spotted Cassie and Alex and waved. "Hello!"

Cassie waved back. "Do you need any help?" she called above the howling wind.

"We're fine, thanks," the woman said with a smile, as she sorted through a box of brushes, combs, bottles, and cloths.

The girl looked over at them. "Hi," she said. "Come and meet my pony."

Cassie went over and stroked the pony's soft silver-gray nose. "He's cute," she said. "What's his name?"

"Sunbeam," said the girl. "And I'm Sita Shah."

As Cassie and Alex introduced themselves,

Sita's mom came over with a handful of pony treats.

"Sunbeam is competing in the Astral-on-Sea Pony Championship this afternoon," she said. "We're staying with Mrs. Cafferty at Starwatcher Towers. Do you know it?"

Cassie laughed. "I live there," she said. "I'm Cassie Cafferty."

"And I'm staying there," said Alex. "It's at the top of the hill. See?" He pointed.

"Gosh!" said Mrs. Shah. "It must be even windier up there."

"I measured the wind speed," Alex said proudly. "It's officially gale force, which is very strong." He helped Mrs. Shah close up the trailer.

★　✳　★　✳

"We'll show you the way to Starwatcher Towers," said Cassie.

"Thanks," said Mrs. Shah, "but Sita needs to exercise Sunbeam first. He has to stretch his legs after our trip."

The pony whinnied softly, and nuzzled Cassie's neck. She giggled. "He's gorgeous," she said. "I bet he'll do well in the competition."

Sita sighed. "I doubt it," she said, and laid her face against the pony's cheek.

"Why?" asked Cassie.

"Sunbeam doesn't like jumping," said Sita, "but he's got to try." She turned to Cassie and whispered, "You see,

Mom used to ride in competitions, but she can't now, because she hurt her back. Sunbeam was born at our stables, and she adores him. If we do well, she'd be so proud and happy." Sita stroked the pony's nose. "Oh, Sunbeam," she said, "I wish we could win the competition."

Cassie smiled. *Aha!* she thought. *I've found someone to help!*

She watched Sita lead Sunbeam to a bucket of fresh water. It would be wonderful to make Sita's wish come true — and then Cassie would earn her next magical charm!

"I have to teach Sunbeam to jump," Cassie murmured to herself. "But how?"

3
Runaway!

Cassie patted Sunbeam's warm neck while Sita gently slipped the bridle over his head. Then Sita saddled the pony. She showed Alex how to fasten the straps underneath Sunbeam's tummy, and how to check that the saddle wasn't too loose or too tight.

"Just right," she said. "Pretty good for your first time, Alex!"

Cassie smiled at her friend. He grinned back happily.

A sudden gust of wind whipped Bert's hat off and flung it through the open gate. He stumbled back against a row of empty feed buckets and sent them clattering across the yard.

The donkeys brayed in surprise. *"Errrgh-hee-errrgh-heee-errrgh!"* At the same time, one of the stable doors banged shut. Sunbeam whirled around and threw his head back in fear. Before anyone could stop him, the terrified pony bolted through the gate and out onto the beach. Within seconds, he was just a spot in the distance.

"Sunbeam!" Sita cried. She ran to the gate. "Mom!" she called. "We have to go after him."

"Wait," Mrs. Shah said. "Let me think! Oh, I don't know what to do! We've never been to Astral-on-Sea before. I don't know where to look. Maybe Bert can help. . . ."

But Bert was busy calming the jittery donkeys. "Let me settle these guys down, and then I'll call around and get people to look for Sunbeam," he said. "I should have shut that gate more tightly. . . ."

"Don't worry, Mrs. Shah!" said Cassie. "Alex and I will find Sunbeam. You and

Sita should drive up to Starwatcher Towers. You get a good view from up on the cliff, so maybe you'll spot him."

With that, she and Alex tore out onto the empty, windswept sand. "We'll find him!" Cassie shouted over her shoulder as she ran.

She knew exactly what to do. She looked down at the tiny bird charm on her bracelet. A tingle ran up her arm and through her whole body, and silvery sparkles danced all around her.

Cassie grabbed Alex's hand. "Hold on!" she called as they rose into the air. She felt as light as a cloud. This was the magic of her bird charm! They flew along the beach, sticking close to the cliff's edge to avoid being spotted.

"Whooooa!" cried Alex.

"You're okay," said Cassie. "You've flown with me before, remember?"

Alex held tightly to her hand. "How could I forget? This is amazing. I can feel air currents moving in different directions."

Cassie smiled. "Forget science, for once. Just enjoy the magic."

Alex laughed. "I'll try!"

A butterfly with pink wings flitted beside them. It did a happy loop in the air, as if it was enjoying the blustery wind, then fluttered away.

A moment later, Cassie spotted something moving near a wooded area at the edge of the beach. "Is that Sunbeam, Alex? Down there, near the trees?"

"Yes!" said Alex. "Let's fly a little lower."

Cassie tugged on Alex's hand, guiding them back to the ground. With a flurry of whirling leaves and silver sparkles, they landed in a small clearing in the woods.

Alex brushed himself off. "The wind's dying down," he said. "Here comes the sun!"

"Never mind the weather," said Cassie. "Where's that runaway pony?"

But Sunbeam was nowhere in sight.

4
Snorter Knows

"Sunbeam! Sunbeam!" Cassie and Alex called. But the pony didn't show himself.

Then Cassie saw something light-colored at the far edge of the woods.

"Look!" she cried, pointing. "There's Sunbeam!"

They raced through the trees and came out into a grassy field dotted with grazing sheep and golden buttercups.

"You must have seen a sheep," said Alex.

"Sunbeam's not here. I'll keep checking in the woods."

The sheep! Of course!

Cassie thought hard about her crescent moon charm. Instantly, the bracelet glowed and silver sparkles streamed from it. They swirled around Cassie's head, flashing in the sunlight.

"Excuse me!" she called.

Sparkles danced toward a big, woolly sheep nearby.

"Are you talking to me?" asked the sheep.

Cassie nodded. It was working! "Has a pretty dappled pony come by here?"

"*Bah!*" said the sheep. "He might be pretty, but he's not very well behaved. He nearly sent my little Baabaa flying." She nodded to a

lamb prancing giddily among the buttercups.

"Which way did the pony go?" asked Cassie.

"Toward the duck pond," said the sheep.

"Thanks!" Cassie said with a wave. She was halfway across the field before she realized that Alex hadn't followed her.

"Come on, Alex!" she called out.

"Cassie, we're not done searching the woods," said Alex, stepping out from among the trees.

"But the sheep said . . ." Cassie stopped and laughed. "Silly me. You couldn't understand her, could you?"

"Understand who?" asked Alex.

"That nice sheep." Cassie jangled her bracelet. "I've been talking to her. Come on, let's go to the duck pond. I'll explain on the way."

But there was no sign of Sunbeam there, either. Cassie crouched down, showering a tiny yellow duckling with silver sparkles. "Have you seen a dappled pony?"

The duckling's eyes opened wide. "Yes.

He drank some of my pond—and he almost drank me up, too!"

"I'm sure he didn't mean it," said Cassie. "Which way did he go?"

"To the pigsty," said the duckling. "He'd better not upset Snorter."

Cassie thanked the duckling and hurried to the pigsty, trailing clouds of silver sparkles. Alex ran after her.

"What now?" said a cranky voice from behind the sty gate.

It was a large pink pig, who snapped at the sparkles that swirled around his nose.

"You must be Snorter," said Cassie.

"If you've come to find that greedy pony,

you're most welcome," said the pig. "Please get him out of our farmyard."

"He's such a sweet pony," said Cassie. "He won't cause any trouble."

Snorter grunted angrily. "Won't cause any trouble?" He stomped a muddy hoof. "That pony ate my lunch!"

Cassie noticed an empty bucket by the pigsty gate. "Oh, no!"

"Is that all you can say?" the pig snorted. "That pony's probably started eating my dinner already, too. Find a wheelbarrow full of apples, and I'll bet you find your pony."

"Alex, look for a wheelbarrow," Cassie instructed.

Alex checked all around the pigsty wall. "Not here," he said. "I'll look behind that barn." A moment later, he yelled, "Cassie, come quick!"

She ran behind the barn and there, munching happily on the apples in the wheelbarrow, was the runaway pony.

"Sunbeam!" Cassie threw her arms around

his neck, sending silver sparkles whirling around them both.

"Uh-oh. Am I in trouble?" neighed the pony.

Cassie stroked him gently. "No, you're not in trouble, Sunbeam."

The pony looked up at her in surprise.

★　✳　★　✳

"Can you understand me? How do you know what I said?"

"It's a long story," said Cassie, "and we have to get back to Sita."

Sunbeam tossed his head.

"What's wrong?" asked Cassie. "You love Sita, don't you?"

"Of course." The pony nodded. "I'll go back, I promise. Later."

Cassie looked into his huge dark eyes. Was it her imagination, or did Sunbeam look sad? "Why did you run away?"

"The bangs and clatters frightened me," he said. "So did the donkeys and their braying."

"But, Sunbeam," said Cassie, "it was just the wind blowing everything around, and the donkeys were scared, too. The wind's died down now, so there's nothing to be scared of anymore."

"Yes, there is." Sunbeam pulled away. "There's . . . the competition."

"Oh, of course," said Cassie. "Sita told me that you don't like jumping."

"I hate it!" Sunbeam neighed. "Jumping *really* scares me."

Cassie stroked his neck softly. *Oh, no,* she thought. *Poor Sunbeam!*

5
Catch the Carrot

Cassie looked at Alex. "We have to help Sunbeam get over his fear of jumping," she whispered. "I really want to make Sita's wish come true."

Before Alex could reply, a cheery voice called out, "Hello, young Cassie."

A smiling, round-faced man came down the path from the farmhouse, carrying a large china bowl.

"Farmer Greg!" Cassie said. "Please

don't be angry, but this pony ate Snorter's
lunch . . . *and* some of his dinner."

"Don't worry. Plenty more
where that came from," said
the farmer with a chuckle.
"Bert called and told me to
watch out for a runaway."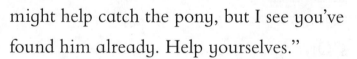
He handed the bowl to
Cassie. It was full of
carrots. "I thought these
might help catch the pony, but I see you've
found him already. Help yourselves."

"Thanks," said Cassie and Alex, each
taking a carrot.

"I saw you talking to the pony, Cassie,"
said Farmer Greg. "It looked like you were
hoping he'd reply!"

"Oh, I was just calming Sunbeam down," Cassie said. She couldn't explain what she was *really* doing. Farmer Greg would never believe her!

The farmer laughed. "Well, keep at it," he said. "With a bit of practice, he might be able to answer you!"

A bit of practice? That gave Cassie an idea. "We'll take Sunbeam back to Bert's stables, but can we use your paddock for a while first, please?"

"Of course you can! If you need riding helmets, there are some in the barn," said Farmer Greg. He put the bowl of carrots on a low wall. "I'm off to check the sheep. Back in a bit."

Cassie found two buckets and took them

into the paddock, where the horses trained. She put the buckets upside down, a few feet apart. "Would you hand me that broom please, Alex?" she called.

As soon as Cassie laid the broom over the buckets, Alex realized what she was doing. "You're making little jumps," he said.

"That's right," said Cassie. Then she whispered, "I know what will tempt that greedy little pony to jump!"

She filled her pockets with carrots, then concentrated hard on her crescent moon charm. Instantly, her arm tingled.

"What are you up to?" asked Alex.

"Watch." Cassie walked over to the pony in a drift of silver sparkles. "Sunbeam, we're going to play Catch the Carrot. Would you like to play, too?"

"I don't know how," said Sunbeam sadly.

"It's easy," said Cassie. "Just copy Alex." She held out a fat carrot and cried, "Come on, Alex, catch the carrot!" Then she ran.

Alex chased after her. As they circled around toward Sunbeam, Cassie slowed down, and Alex grabbed the carrot.

"I win!" he said, and took a big crunchy bite. "Yummy!"

Sunbeam trotted to Cassie. "Can I play now?" he asked.

"Okay." She waved a carrot in front of his

nose. "Go!" She ran off and the pony trotted after her. As she reached the first jump, she thought about her bird charm. She tingled from head to toe, silver sparkles swirled around her, and she took off. *Wheee!* She floated over the broom.

But Sunbeam stopped. He wouldn't jump.

Cassie floated back and forth over the broom a couple of times. "This is fun!" she cried, waving the carrot. "Yum!"

This time, Sunbeam trotted toward the jump — and leaped right over it!

Hooray! thought Cassie. *One more time . . .*

Sunbeam followed her over the next jump, too!

Cassie decided he deserved a reward, so she let him catch the carrot. It was gone in a flash!

★ ✳ ★ ✳

"Let's play again!" said Sunbeam, neighing with excitement.

"Okay." Cassie floated over the jumps, while the pony leaped after her.

The next time he caught a carrot, he said, "I didn't know jumping could be so much fun!"

While Sunbeam crunched on his snack, Alex whispered, "Don't feed him any more, or he'll be too full to jump in the competition."

"You're right," said Cassie. "Let's take him back to the stables. Sita will be so worried, and she'll need time to get him ready." She paused. "There's just one problem. I don't think I can fly with you *and* Sunbeam. Even if I could, we don't want anyone to see us."

"But it will take forever to walk back,"

said Alex. He glanced at his watch. "The competition starts in an hour."

Cassie stroked the pony's silky mane. "How are we going to get back in time?"

Sunbeam's ears twitched. "I've got an idea!"

Sunbeam Takes Charge

"I'm strong," Sunbeam said. "I'll give you both a ride. If I trot all the way back to the stables, we'll be there in no time."

"You smart little pony!" Cassie cried.

"What did he say?" Alex looked confused.

"We can both ride Sunbeam back to the stables," said Cassie. Then she stopped and thought. "But I've never ridden a pony before."

"Me neither," said Alex, suddenly looking worried.

Cassie spoke to Sunbeam again. "We don't know what to do," said Cassie. "It's a little bit scary to ride on a pony."

"You helped me be brave," said Sunbeam. "Now I'll help you! All you need are riding helmets."

"Farmer Greg said we could borrow some," said Cassie. She ran into the barn and found two black helmets. She and Alex put them on.

"Fasten the strap under your chin," said Sunbeam.

Cassie did.

"You, too, Alex," said the pony. But Alex didn't move.

Cassie giggled. "Sorry, Sunbeam, I keep forgetting that I'm the only one who can understand you." She showed Alex how to fasten his hat.

Sunbeam trotted to a low wall. "Stand on that, then climb up onto my back. You first, Cassie, then Alex behind you. Hang on tight."

Once they'd climbed up, Cassie couldn't believe how high they were!

"Take the reins," said Sunbeam, "but don't pull. I'll do all the work. Off we go!"

As he walked forward, Cassie felt Alex hold on to her waist. She gripped the front of the saddle.

"Relax," said Sunbeam. "You'll enjoy it.
Oh, I wish I had a carrot," he muttered.

Cassie giggled. "I heard that!"

"I'm going to trot now," said Sunbeam.
"It'll feel strange at first, but you won't fall,
I promise."

"We're going to go faster, Alex," Cassie
warned. "Hang on!"

His arms tightened around her middle as Sunbeam trotted along. "I'm going to fall off!" cried Alex.

"You won't," Cassie promised.

Soon, they got used to the jogging motion, moving up and down to Sunbeam's rhythm.

"Look!" said Alex, suddenly. "There's Bert's hat—over on that wall."

Cassie asked Sunbeam to go to the stone wall. The pony had to hop over a little ditch to get there.

"Whoa!" cried Alex.

"Great jump!" said Cassie.

Alex leaned over and grabbed the hat. "The wind brought it all this way!" he said as Sunbeam trotted on.

Just before they reached the stables, Cassie spotted something shining in a hedge nearby. "The crown!" she cried. "Stop, Sunbeam!"

"A silver crown stuck in a hedge?" said Alex. "Where did that come from?"

Cassie grinned. "The crown is Stella Starkeeper's. It blew off when she came to see me." She leaned over to pick it up, but she couldn't reach.

"I'll get it," said Alex. He slid off Sunbeam's back and passed the crown to Cassie. "You can wear it home!"

Cassie thought
the crown looked
much too big, but she
tried it on anyway.
A tingle ran
through her.

"It fits!" she cried.
That's magic, too, she
thought.

Mrs. Shah's car was just pulling into the
stables as they arrived. Sita leaped out.
"Sunbeam!" she cried.

"There's my Sita," said the pony. "Hold
tight!" He ran even faster. They reached the
gate in a flash! Sunbeam nuzzled Sita's neck,
and she hugged him happily.

"Thank you so much for bringing him

back," she said, looking up at Cassie and
Alex. "How did you find him?"

"Well . . ." Cassie shrugged and grinned at
Alex. "I just asked around!"

★ 7 ★
The Final Round

Cassie and Alex were thrilled when Mrs. Shah invited them to the Pony Championship. They raced up the hill to Starwatcher Towers to change, and Cassie stowed Stella's crown in her nightstand drawer for safekeeping.

Ten minutes later, Mr. and Mrs. Cafferty waved good-bye as Cassie and Alex drove off beside Sita in the backseat of the big green truck, with Sunbeam in the trailer behind them.

Sita was quiet. Cassie touched her arm.
"Are you okay?"

"I'm nervous," Sita said. "I'm afraid that
Sunbeam will refuse to jump. I really want
to win a prize."

Mrs. Shah smiled. "Winning is a bonus.
It's trying that's important, sweetie."

"I know," Sita said in a small voice. "But
I want to win." She turned to Cassie and
whispered, "For Mom."

Cassie crossed her fingers.

When they reached the showground, everyone helped groom Sunbeam. Sita cleaned any spots of mud off his body, and Cassie brushed his glossy mane. Then Sita showed her how to use a smooth, damp cloth to remove dust from the pony's coat and give it an extra shine. Alex helped Mrs. Shah put oil on Sunbeam's hooves.

As Cassie brushed Sunbeam's mane, he leaned his head against her.

"He likes you," said Sita.

"I like him, too," said Cassie. "I'm beginning to understand ponies."

Alex spluttered with laughter, but no one noticed because there was an announcement over the speaker system: *The competition starts in five minutes.*

"I'll be right back!" Sita cried, grabbing a bag from the car. She disappeared into the horse trailer. Soon she came out wearing a black jacket and hat, cream-colored riding pants, and shiny boots. Cassie gasped. "You look fantastic!" she cried. "I don't know who looks better, you or Sunbeam," Sita's mom said, smiling.

Cassie could see that Mrs. Shah was proud of Sita. *I hope she'll be just as proud of Sunbeam,* she thought.

Sita slipped her foot into one of the stirrups that hung from Sunbeam's saddle. She swung into the saddle and rode off to line up for the competition.

"Good luck, Sita!" Cassie and Alex cried. "Good luck, Sunbeam!"

They headed for the roped-off arena where the show-jumping course was set up with colorful jumps — a stack of hay bales, a wooden fence, and a log lying across a pair of sturdy posts. Some spectators had folding chairs or blankets to sit on while they watched. On the far side of the arena, the

judges sat at a long table. Ponies and riders waited nervously outside for their turn.

When the announcer said, "Next is Sita Shah and Sunbeam," Cassie held her breath.

Sunbeam entered the ring, the starting bell rang, and they were off! The first jump was low, so he sailed over it.

Cassie heard Mrs. Shah gasp in surprise as the brave little pony cleared jump after jump. "Only two to go," she said.

Sunbeam jumped again.

"Just one more," said Alex.

"Come on, Sunbeam," Cassie murmured.

But the pony's hind leg caught a striped
pole and sent it
clattering to the
ground. A groan
went up from the
crowd.

"Just one jump down
for Sita and Sunbeam," said the announcer.
"Maybe we'll see you in the second round."

Mrs. Shah explained that if no one got
a perfect round, then those who had only
knocked down one fence would go again to
see who was the winner.

At the end of the first round, the judge

announced that there would be a jump-off between Sunbeam and two other ponies.

Sita rode over. "Wasn't Sunbeam wonderful?" she said. "He's so brave. It almost felt like he was enjoying himself!"

"I think he was," said Cassie with a grin. Sita frowned and said, "I hope knocking that fence down doesn't throw him off in the next round." Cassie had been wondering the same thing. She had to give the pony a pep talk! "Should I take Sunbeam to get a drink of water?" she suggested.

$\star$ $\ast$ $\bigstar$ $\ast$

"Good idea," said Sita. "Thanks! But don't let him have too much, or he won't feel like jumping."

Cassie led the pony away, thinking hard about her crescent moon charm. Silver sparkles swirled around Sunbeam's head.

"You were wonderful!" she told him.

"Thanks. I liked knowing you were watching," said Sunbeam. "It made me feel braver."

Cassie patted his neck as he drank. "You'll enjoy the next round," she said, "because now you *know* you can do it."

* ✳ ★ ✦

"Cassie! It's my turn!" called Sita. "Quick!"

With a whispered "Go for it!" Cassie led the pony over to Sita. She climbed up into the saddle, and Sunbeam trotted over to the starting place.

"The other two ponies have taken their turns," said Mrs. Shah. Her eyes shone. "They both knocked down a fence, so if Sunbeam clears all his jumps, he and Sita will win!"

They all leaned on the gate to watch. Cassie was so nervous for Sita that she could barely breathe. Had her Lucky Star magic been enough?

Sunbeam's tail flew as he jumped the first four fences perfectly. And the next! And

the next! Soon, there was only one fence left—the fence he'd knocked down in the first round.

"I can't look," said Cassie. But she did.

Sunbeam leaped into the air and—oh, no! His hoof touched the pole. It rattled and shook, but didn't fall. He made it over the fence!

"He did it!" yelled Alex.

Everyone cheered!

"The winner, with the only clear round," said the announcer, "is Sita Shah, on the magnificent Sunbeam!"

When the blue ribbon was clipped onto Sunbeam's bridle, Sita beamed at her mom. Cassie thought that neither of them could look any happier.

Her arm tingled. She looked down to see her bracelet glowing brightly. As the glow faded, it revealed a shiny new charm—a delicate butterfly with shimmering pink wings.

It's like the butterfly that flew next to us while we were looking for Sunbeam, Cassie thought, thrilled. *I wonder what magic power it will give me.*

★ ★ ★

At bedtime, Cassie glanced around her room. It was circular, and there were stars everywhere—on her bedding, on her rug,

and even on her purple pajamas. Her moon-
shaped bedside lamp shone softly on the
starry wallpaper.

I've always loved stars, she thought, *and now
that I've met Stella Starkeeper, they're even more
important to me.*

She snuggled into bed with Twinkle curled
up beside her, and gazed up at the night sky
through the open panel in her glass ceiling.
Thousands of stars were sprinkled across the
sky. But one glowed brighter than the rest.

★ ✳ ★ ✳

She sat up, her bracelet sparkling. "Twinkle, look!"

The old cat stirred. "I'd rather snooze, thanks," he murmured.

Cassie slipped out of bed and took Stella's crown from her nightstand drawer. She thought hard about her bird charm . . . and floated up through the open panel, into the dark and starry sky.

She flew toward the brightest star. As she got closer, the light softened and changed into a silver-haired woman in a shimmering dress.

"Look what I found," cried Cassie, holding out the crown.

Stella Starkeeper smiled. "I thought I'd lost it," she said. "You not only helped Sita

today, but you helped Sunbeam, too—and now you've helped me. You're going to make a wonderful Lucky Star!"

"I hope so," said Cassie.

"You've earned your third charm," Stella said, touching Cassie's bracelet. "You only need four more. Now go home and get some sleep. You'll need it for your next adventure. Starry dreams!"

* ✳ ★ ✳

Cassie yawned, stretched, and drifted down toward Starwatcher Towers, wondering about the butterfly charm. What new adventure would it bring?

She couldn't wait to find out!

Make Your Own!

You can talk to animals, too, just like Cassie! Here's how to make a fun animal hand puppet that might even talk back:

You Need:

- One spare sock or mitten
- White chalk
- Felt in different colors
- Scissors
- Fabric glue

★ ✳ ★ ✳

1. Choose what animal you'd like to make! You could try a cat (like Twinkle), a dog (like Comet), a horse (like Sunbeam), or any other animal you can think of.

2. Using the chalk, draw shapes for eyes, nose, ears, paws, and whiskers (if needed) onto the felt.

3. With an adult's help, use scissors to carefully cut out the felt shapes.

4. Glue the felt pieces to your sock or mitten! The nose should go front and center, with the other pieces arranged around it.

5. Put your hand inside your sock or mitten, and make your new pet talk!

Can Cassie make another wish come true?

Take a sneak peek at

#3: Wish Upon a Song!

✦ 1 ✦
Songs on the Sand

"*Magic, magic moments, these are magic moments . . .*" Cassie sang.

"*Yowl, yowl, meow, yowl . . .*" Her black-and-white cat, Twinkle, joined in.

Their voices echoed in the huge observatory dome at Starwatcher Towers. Cassie was singing along to "Magic Moments," the latest hit by Jacey Day. She was Cassie's favorite pop star! In fact, that afternoon Cassie and her friend Kate were going to watch Jacey perform. She was the opening act in the Songs on the Sand music festival, right in their own town of Astral-on-Sea!

★　　✳　　★　　✳

All week, Cassie and Kate had been practicing a special dance routine to "Magic Moments." As she twirled around, Cassie imagined that Kate was dancing in the Fairy Cupcake Bakery where she lived with her mom.

Cassie turned up the music. "Let's dance, Twinkle!" She giggled.

Twinkle blinked his eyes. Cassie scooped him up from the old leather chair where he sat and spun around, being careful not to bump into any of the shiny telescopes. Her dad was an astronomer. Most nights he could be found up here in the observatory, watching the stars.

"There's a friend I'd love to meet
Spinning world beneath his feet,

He's got pebbles in his hands
Running 'cross the glistening sands. . . ."

Along with Jacey's sweet, clear voice, the backup singers added a catchy harmony to the song. The sound of their voices blending together made Cassie want to sing and dance!

When the song ended, Cassie noticed a tingling feeling in her arm. She put Twinkle back on the chair and looked at the charm bracelet around her wrist. Her new butterfly charm seemed to flutter its colorful wings.

"I wonder what magical power this charm has," Cassie said, "and who I'll help next."

Cassie used her charms to help make people's wishes come true! With each person that she helped, she received another magic

★　＊　★　＊

charm for her bracelet. So far, Cassie had three. The bird charm gave her the power to fly, and the crescent moon allowed her to talk to animals. But she still wasn't sure what the butterfly charm did. She couldn't wait to find out!

RAINBOW magic™

There's Magic in Every Series!

The Rainbow Fairies

The Weather Fairies

The Jewel Fairies

The Pet Fairies

The Fun Day Fairies

The Petal Fairies

The Dance Fairies

The Music Fairies

The Sports Fairies

The Party Fairies

The Ocean Fairies

The Night Fairies

The Magical Animal Fairies

Read them all!

📖 SCHOLASTIC

www.scholastic.com

www.rainbowmagiconline.com

HIT entertainment

RMFAIRY5

KITTY CORNER

Where kitties get the love they need

KITTY CORNER
Where kitties get the love they need

CALLIE

ELLEN MILES
SCHOLASTIC

KITTY CORNER
Where kitties get the love they need

OTIS

ELLEN MILES
SCHOLASTIC

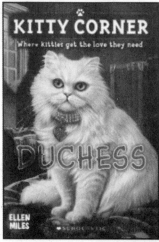

KITTY CORNER
Where kitties get the love they need

DUCHESS

ELLEN MILES
SCHOLASTIC

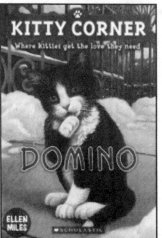

KITTY CORNER
Where kitties get the love they need

DOMINO

ELLEN MILES
SCHOLASTIC

These purr-fect kittens need a home!

SCHOLASTIC